Also by Daniel Kehlmann

F

Fame

Me and Kaminski

Measuring the World

You Should Have Left

You Should Have Left

Daniel Kehlmann

Translated from the German by Ross Benjamin

Pantheon Books, New York

Translation copyright © 2017 by Ross Benjamin

All rights reserved. Published in the United States by Pantheon Books, a division of Penguin Random House LLC, New York, and distributed in Canada by Random House of Canada, a division of Penguin Random House Canada Limited, Toronto. Originally published in hardcover in Germany as *Du hättest gehen sollen* by Rowohlt Verlag GmbH, Reinbeck bei Hamburg, in 2016. Copyright © 2016 by Rowohlt Verlag GmbH, Reinbeck bei Hamburg.

Pantheon Books and colophon are registered trademarks of Penguin Random House LLC.

Library of Congress Cataloging-in-Publication Data
Names: Kehlmann, Daniel, [date] author. Benjamin, Ross, translator.
Title: You should have left / Daniel Kehlmann ; translated from the German by Ross Benjamin.
Other titles: Du hattest gehen sollen. English.
Description: First American edition. New York : Pantheon, 2017.
Identifiers: LCCN 2016043779 (print). LCCN 2016048424 (ebook).
ISBN 9781101871928 (hardcover). ISBN 9781101871980 (ebook)
Subjects: LCSH: Authors—Germany—Fiction. Psychological fiction.
BISAC: FICTION / Literary. FICTION / Ghost. FICTION / Visionary & Metaphysical.
Classification: LCC PT2671.E32 D813 2017 (print). LCC PT2671.E32 (ebook). DDC 833/.914—dc23
LC record available at lccn.loc.gov/2016043779

www.pantheonbooks.com

Jacket design by Peter Mendelsund

Printed in the United States of America

First American Edition

9 8 7 6 5 4 3 2 1

You Should Have Left

December 2

Jana and Ella are riding a tandem bike along a country road. The sun is shining, the stalks are swaying, cheerful music. Ella at the helm, Jana spreads her arms. Close-up: She blinks happily into the sun. Then the bike runs over a rock, goes off the road, and falls over. Cries of pain. The music breaks off, fade to black, opening credits.

Immediately sets the right tone.

It's fitting that I'm beginning a new notebook up here. New surroundings, new ideas, a new beginning. Fresh air.

Last week Esther turned four. Everything's getting easier now. It's already noticeable that there's no longer constant arguing over who's getting up with her, who's putting her to bed, who's playing blocks or trains or Legos. She can do a lot more by herself.

The cold blue-white of the two glaciers, under them sheer granite, then the woods, which the haze turns into a smooth dark-green surface. The sky is lightly clouded, a cloud has drifted in front of the sun, its frayed white edges are outlined in fire.

Outside the house that we've rented, the meadow slopes gently for about a hundred yards to the edge of the woods: spruces, pines, and, at the edge, a huge, pale willow. When I open the window I hear the wind whispering. Apart from that I hear nothing. Far below lies the valley with its dice-sized houses, cut through by three ribbons: road, river, railroad. Branching off, like a thin pencil stroke, is the road on which we came up.

A terrible drive, by the way. That road is steep, with many hairpin bends and no side barriers, and Susanna is a horrendous driver. It was hard for me not to say anything. Well, and then, unfortunately, I did say something, and so we yelled at each other the rest of the way.

The sun has just pushed its way out from behind the cloud, so that the sky is now melting in painful, blazing, magnificent brilliance.

Or is that too many metaphors? The sun doesn't push its way anywhere, the wind pushes the cloud away, and of course the sky by no means melts. But *in painful, blazing, magnificent brilliance*, not bad.

For once it's a house that looks even better in reality than in the pictures on the Internet. Not a musty little Alpine hut, but two stories, new, and minimalist, with a narrow upper balcony and a large living-room window, clearly an architect-designed house.

> piercing brilliance
> fiery cloud
> the sun rolling through the firmament
> mountains, engraved in the blue

Firmament—antiquated. Better just to go with the plain word *sky*. Have a minor character use the word *firmament* twice. That's all you need, you've established that character.

Fade-in, Jana is walking down the street, carrying a shopping

Just as I was about to keep writing, they came in. And when they're in the room, I can't focus. Now they're playing on the carpet and being loud, and I keep scribbling so that they think I'm working, because if Susanna doesn't think that I'm working, she'll just say once again: Stop complaining, you're not working anyway, so I write and write and write and act as if I were busy, and I actually am busy, because ultimately the whole production is waiting for me.

I love her, and I don't want any other life. Why do we fight all the time?

Again just now. She stood up reproachfully from the carpet, and I thought: Here we go.

And she really said exactly what I had known she was going to say: We just got here, do you really immediately have to, couldn't you first spend a little time with, etc.

Then nothing will get done, I said. That's not how art is created!

You mean your *screenplay*?

It was the emphasis she put on the word. She knows exactly what most makes me angry. And of course I walked into the trap. A screenplay not art? I cried. *La Strada, Barry Lyndon*—not art?

Her completely calm reply: A screenplay is art, but not *art*. Not the way you say it. And *Besties 2*, well . . .

Someday I'll write a movie about all this. Long dialogues, lots of flashbacks, no music. It will be called *Marriage*. The title hasn't been used yet; astonishingly, it's available.

I shouldn't have responded. If I'd just kept my mouth shut, the fight could have been avoided.

But I couldn't resist reminding her that the

royalties for those screenplays that she might have considered art but not *art*, and indeed especially the *Besties* screenplay, are paying the mortgage for our house, a town house with a backyard, which she considers so important because a child has to have a backyard, after all, and now we have the town house, and the mortgage is far from paid off, and Esther actually never plays in the backyard, and if I don't write the sequel to my most successful movie, what about the mortgage then?

To which she replied that she had nothing against my comedies, as long as I please wouldn't act as if they were *Twelfth Night* or *The Importance of Being Earnest*—she always has to bring up classics to remind me that she has a degree in comp lit and classical studies, whereas I've never attended a university— and by the way, my affectation of writing by hand as if I were a poet was insufferable. Then she took a step back and laughed as cuttingly as only actors can, when they're having an off day. It sounded so artificial that I shuddered, and at that very moment we were interrupted, because Esther had broken the arm off her doll and was bawling and demanding glue, and where are we supposed to get glue up here?

Now they're bending down over the parts of the doll and pushing them around and waiting for a miracle, and I keep writing and don't look up, so that it's clear that I'm too busy to help with that nonsense.

Marriage. The secret is that you love each other anyway. I wouldn't want to be without her—I'd even miss her actor's laugh. And she wouldn't want to be without me. If only we didn't get on each other's nerves so much.

Get away, while

December 3

Before everything could get better yesterday, the kid had to be put to bed. Reconciliation is never conceivable as long as the kid is awake.

Then we stood side by side at the living-room window and looked out into the night: thousands upon thousands of crystal-clear points in the black velvet, below them the contours of the two glaciers faintly glowing, and behind our house there must have been an especially full moon, because the slope in front of us was almost as bright as day from the white light.

On the way to the bedroom we briefly got lost, because we didn't know the house yet, and we ended up in a storeroom with a washing machine and dryer. A vacuum cleaner leaning against the wall crashed down. We listened with bated breath, but Esther hadn't woken up.

Slapstick, said Susanna. Things have a life of their own.

I don't like slapstick, I said.

A little bit of slapstick isn't bad, she said. Would you like me to show you?

Then we went upstairs and found our bedroom.

The main characters are well established by the first movie, but now the sequel has to add backstory.

Flashback to childhood? Old trick, conventional, reliable, but the truth is, I know nothing about Jana's or Ella's childhood. I told the students at the film academy last year that you should know everything about your characters, especially where and how they grew up, but I only said it because it's in the textbooks. I don't have the slightest idea what happened in

Jana's or Ella's childhood, and it doesn't interest me either. Which is why I also don't know
how Jana reacts when Ella asks her to move
out of her apartment, where Jana was living
in the previous movie, so that Ella's new boy-
friend can move in—who is none other than
Jana's ex-boyfriend Martin, with whom she
broke up only because he's a senior tax official.
He's good-looking, sensitive, and well-read, he
speaks several languages, but, as Jana explained
so eloquently at the time, who wants to be in a
relationship with a tax official?

Something strange just happened.

So how does Jana react? We know how impul-
sive she is. Everyone remembers her fit of rage
in the first movie when, out of the blue, she told
the gym teacher that people like him lend the
word *stupidity* new majesty. Something like that
has to happen again, but differently, because
everyone's waiting for it. What happens when
she, whose biggest problem is her lack of self-

control, is suddenly thrown out—in the nicest possible way—of her best friend's apartment?

Must have been mistaken.

Don't think about it.

It's completely quiet now; so quiet that the silence itself seems to be faintly rushing. Probably the blood in my ears.

The living room looks like most living rooms that have been done in recent years by interior designers: parquet floor, white walls, flat ceiling lamps, large kitchen with stainless steel surfaces and center island. In the middle is the wooden table from which I'm looking out the huge glass window into the darkening afternoon, watching Susanna and Esther build stone heaps in the meadow while their breath turns into little vapor clouds. They should be able to see me too, I'm sitting as if on a stage. In front of me, translucent, my reflection: glasses, hair, and collar, the notebook on the table, the pen in my hand. All there again. It was my imagination. What else.

This time Jana remains calm. That's it! Everyone's expecting the fit of rage, but it doesn't come!

Ella tells Jana to move out. Jana's composure is so surprising that Ella feels provoked by it.

E: You didn't even want to live here anymore!

J: Where did you get that idea?

E: It's obvious. Because you're smiling like that. Why are you smiling?

J: Because you've found Mr. Right.

E: What are you implying?

J: What do you mean?

E: Is it because he works for the tax office?

J: It's a job like any other job.

E: Exactly.

J: The state can't function without tax officials.

E: That's just the tone I mean!

J: There wouldn't be any streets, and in the streets, which wouldn't exist, there would be anarchy. We broke up because he wasn't right for me. But he's clearly right for you.

And at that very moment Martin comes in, wearing a suit and carrying a briefcase under his arm, and Ella, who doesn't know where to direct her rage, begins to scream at him under some pretext, and Jana stands there—

> not smiling
> sadly
> no, expressionlessly

—yes, much better: She stands there expressionlessly, her face doesn't betray whether she intentionally started a fight between the two of them or whether she really meant everything.

Although, if he comes in just at that moment, it looks too much like a sitcom, that's totally cheap. Get away. But if not him, then who? Someone should come in.

Now they're walking back to the house. Susanna is texting: The bright screen of the phone casts its glow on her face. The little one has something in her hand. Apparently she found something on the ground. She always finds something.

I have to tell Schmidt the idea of Jana remaining calm, he'll like that. He's definitely going to call soon. He knows that I'm here to work and is waiting for the screenplay. Just recently he hinted that if necessary, the production company, which owns the rights to the material, will have to avail themselves of the help of another writer, of course you're the best, who else could do it, our first choice of course, completely irreplaceable, but the sequel has to be shot, the success of *Besties* demands it, and if you don't deliver, what else can we do! Then he added that it's not up to him, he would wait for me forever. But the producers! He said this so convincingly, so warmheartedly and full of friendship, that the objection that he himself was the producer didn't even occur to me until after we had hung up.

———

Esther showed me what she found outside. It was a rock that looked like any other rock, and I exclaimed Oh! and Ah! and Wonderful! Then I gave her a kiss, her skin was still cold from the evening air.

Looks like a diamond, she said.

That's true, I replied, that's really true! Like a diamond.

Now I'm going to the kitchen to make dinner.

December 4

Yesterday was the best evening in a very long time. Except for that dream.

I had volunteered to put Esther to bed, read her a picture book about a mouse that finds out that the moon is made of cheese. The mouse eats the moon, but afterward it's still there, and then the mouse falls asleep, and that's the end of the book. My daughter liked the nonsense, and I liked that she liked it, and she snuggled up to me, and the night snuggled up to the window, and when I turned out the light, I saw the glaciers in the distance, and a few minutes later I heard her regular breathing.

After the fight a scene in which Martin goes to the office and is somehow dissatisfied with himself. He looks around, he suddenly recognizes in his colleagues what others see in him: tax officials. And he is one of them. How could it have happened that he became a tax official? On the computer he looks at pictures from his school days. Back then he wasn't a tax official yet. Then pictures from his university days, which show him wearing a tie, show him solving crossword puzzles with an expression that's serious, even devoted: The transformation has begun. He looks down at himself. He loosens his tie, immediately feels insecure, tightens it again. Distractedly he flips through a magazine, stops at a picture of a pop singer who is standing in a particularly casual manner, his hair tousled, his shirt open to his belly button, metal rings on his fingers. He hesitates for a few seconds, then he reaches for the telephone, orders a tax audit of the singer, and slowly and deliberately loosens his tie.

After Esther had fallen asleep, I walked on tiptoe out of the room. Oddly, I got lost again, the corridor suddenly seemed longer to me, and yet I'd had only one glass of wine. I discovered that there are a further three bedrooms; the house is much too big for the three of us. I'm surprised that it's not more expensive.

Then we sat until two o'clock in the morning at the table and drank wine and talked. Just like in the old days. Like nine years ago, when we first met on Schmidt's set. I had never seen such an exciting woman before. Susanna, in case you're reading this, which I suspect you aren't, because my work doesn't particularly interest you, then you should know, it's true: never in my life! I wanted to touch you and kiss you and know everything about you, wanted to spend my life with you.

And I, she said last night at the table, couldn't have imagined the day when I'd be yelling at you about diapers or arguing with you about how much to pay babysitters.

But that's probably as it should be, I said, because I couldn't think of anything else to say.

The natural course of things, she said, and

then she added something in Latin that began with *Nihil toto* or something like that, which annoyed me, but I didn't let it show.

Ovid, she said. Actually Heraclitus's words, but Ovid puts them in Pythagoras's mouth: There's nothing in the world that stays the way it is.

I tried to think about Heraclitus's wise words, but I found it hard, because the quote mainly reminded me that she has a university education and I don't. But at that moment it almost didn't matter.

And so we thought together back to what it had been like when we had first met: everything as always, everything as if for the first time, candlelight and narrow glasses and this and that bar, the movies, the theater, finally your apartment and then my apartment and then yours again; everything as usual, everything as never.

I have to remember the role for Brent Kent. Schmidt is beside himself with joy that he accepted. So there has to be an American in it. I just hope that they don't dub Kent. A dubbed character whose lips don't match the words, when none of the other people are dubbed, that won't work. Schmidt has to promise me that. Kent could be an IRS employee, a colleague of Martin's, from Illinois.

Why Illinois?

Why not.

I could hardly believe, back then, that I of all people should be chosen by this beautiful, famous, mysterious actress. Of course, I wasn't unknown either. Everyone was expecting that I would soon take the step from writing to my directorial debut. That's where the career path of a successful screenwriter usually leads.

Well, that's not how it worked out for me.

But last night, when we sat at the large living-room table until two o'clock with the screen of the baby monitor next to us—though we don't actually need it, because the little one is not a baby anymore and can come to us if she's afraid—we talked and talked, and sometimes your phone buzzed softly, as if talking to itself, and in the valley the lights glowed until they went out one after another, and then we went to bed as in our best days.

Ella and Martin early in the morning. She's asleep, he's looking at her, suddenly she moves. She awakens, he quickly closes his eyes, she opens hers. She looks at him, then she looks around the room. Her clothes are lying untidily on the floor, his neatly folded on the chair, his tie, also folded, on top. Some time passes. Finally, he moves, acts as if he were waking up. But she has closed her eyes again. Taken aback, he looks at her, then he uneasily closes his eyes again. So they lie next to each other and pretend to be asleep. Slow fade-out.

I don't understand why I had a dream like that after such a blissful evening.

An empty room. A naked lightbulb on the ceiling, in the corner a chair with only three legs, one of them broken off. The door was locked; what was I afraid of?

The woman. Her narrow eyes were very close together, on either side of the root of her nose, which had a deep wrinkle down the middle. Her forehead too was wrinkled, and her lips were slightly open, so that I could see her teeth, yellowish like those of heavy smokers. But it was her eyes that were awful.

She stood there while my fear grew unbearable. I was trembling, I had difficulty breathing, my eyes were watering, my legs went weak—this didn't actually happen to my real body, of course, so is it possible that I wasn't afraid at all, that it was only my dream self, just as only my dream hands were trembling? No, the fear was as real as fear can be, and burned in me, and when it was no longer tolerable, the woman took a step back, as if she were releasing me, and only then was I back in our bedroom, where I heard Susanna's steady breathing and saw the moonlight falling softly through the window, and the baby monitor showed our daughter in a deep sleep.

Breakfast: Bright grass and even brighter sun, no clouds, the air full of birds whose names I don't know; I've always regretted that I can't identify birds by name. The way they let the wind carry them, as effortlessly as if flying were the norm, as if it took hard work to stay on the ground.

At the moment Susanna is reading to Esther for the thousandth time from the book about the mouse and the cheese moon, the little one is laughing and clapping, and I'm quickly finishing my writing before I head out. We're running low on provisions, someone has to go down to the village, and I volunteered. Get away. Susanna said thank you and held my hand, and I looked into her eyes. They're not actually blue, more turquoise, with a sprinkling of black.

Will you read me your new scenes?

You don't really want me to.
Don't be so sensitive, of course I do.
I don't have much yet.

It just dawned on me where I know the terri-
fying woman from. I saw her in the photo on
the wall in the laundry room—just to the right
of the Miele washing machine and the dryer,
I noticed it on the first day. But to get night-
mares from that is really too much.

Most people think of themselves as good driv-
ers. Not me. I'm clumsy and absentminded
and have slow reflexes. Whenever I drive, even
under the best conditions, I have the feeling of
letting myself in for something reckless. So it's
not surprising when I'm overcome with panic
on a narrow road of hairpin bends.

This is how it is: You have to be completely
unimaginative to sit down without fear in a
fuel-filled capsule. One second you're firmly
ensconced in everyday life and thinking about
dinner and your tax return, the next you're

wedged in deformed metal while the flames devour you, and all that lies between the one state and the other is a clumsy turn of the steering wheel, half a second of inattention. But I didn't want to be someone who can't cope with everyday life. People have simply agreed that driving a car is something harmless.

I saw Esther and Susanna shrinking in the rearview mirror, the parking area next to the house receded, then the first hairpin bend carried me away. The sun was blinding, and the valley sprang from my right side to my left and, at the next hairpin bend, back again. I broke out in a sweat.

At the next turn the car slid too far out, I stepped on the brake, it came to a stop just in time. Was I too close to the edge of the road? There was no barrier. I put the car in reverse, rolled backward, slowly started driving again. Fortunately, no one was watching me. The next turn was as tight as the previous one, the valley swung from my right side to my left, again I braked, stopped, and started driving once more, tried to stay to the right of the median strip but failed on the first attempt—drive slowly, I thought, there's no rush, you just have to survive. The sun was blinding. Sweat was running down my face. The next turn wasn't too bad, and I noticed an old barn on the roadside, the roof caved-in, the windows empty holes, but I had already been distracted for too long, and the abyss came so close that I cried out. I stepped on the brake with all my strength, then I started driving again.

Thirty minutes later I arrived in the village. There was only one street and only one shop, Gruntner's General Store, across from the church. I stayed in the car for a while with trembling hands and listened to my heartbeat gradually slowing back down.

It's not a pretty village. The houses are low and appear to be cowering. The roofs are pointed, the windows tiny, gray walls, flaking plaster, a bus stop under a gloomy rain shelter, tracks but no train station, because the train doesn't stop here.

A bell announced me when I entered the store: A small room with a counter and a cash register. After a few seconds a door opened and a fat man with bags under his eyes shuffled in. His face seemed to be kneaded out of red dough. He leaned on the counter and eyed me.

I took out the shopping list. Butter, I said, bread and—

With a wave of his hand he cut me short and went out. I heard him rummaging and coughing. After an eternity he came back and put a slab of butter in tinfoil on the counter.

And bread, I said. And eggs and—

He went out. I listened. He rummaged. Something fell on the floor. He cursed softly, then he coughed. Finally, he returned with a misshapen loaf of bread.

I closed my eyes and said: Eggs. Again I heard the door, then his coughing from the next room. I looked at the time on my phone. I had been there for fifteen minutes already.

Bit by bit we worked through the list. He fetched one item at a time, and even though they were the most common foods, he searched for some of them for so long that you might have thought no one had ever asked for them before. He brought plastic-wrapped sausage and a few gnarled apples and two very spotted bananas and ground coffee and coffee filters and milk, and finally I said: Thank you, that's everything.

He nodded, pointed to a spot above my head, and asked: You're staying up there?

It took me a moment to realize that the gesture was directed at our vacation house. Determined to match him in taciturnity, I nodded.

Ah, he said.

Yes, I said.

Well, he said.

Right, I said.

Anything happen yet?

Excuse me?

He was silent.

What should have happened?

You rented?

I nodded.

From Steller?

Is that the owner?

Steller, he said.

Is that the owner's name?

Well, Steller, he said in a tone as if it were impossible that there were people in the world to whom the name meant nothing.

Never heard the name, I said. We rented through Airbnb. I saw his look and added: Internet.

The door to the street opened, and a woman came in who was so small that she hardly came up to my chest. She had short white hair and was wearing huge sunglasses.

He greeted her—or at least I assume he did, I didn't understand what he said, because he had immediately lapsed into dialect. Fehringer has to play him, I thought. I can use all this, and Fehringer would be perfect!

She returned his greeting, or at least I assume she did. Then she spoke for a while in dialect.

When she was finished, he nodded, said: Yes, that's true, or something like that, and shuffled out.

We heard him rummaging.

The woman said something without looking at me. Since no one else was in the room, I had to assume that she had spoken to me.

Excuse me?

She said something again.

Excuse me?

She was silent.

The door opened, and he came back. His face was even redder, and he was breathing heavily. In his hand he was holding a packet of butter wrapped in tinfoil. The woman took it. He said something, she replied, both of them laughed. She left the store without paying.

So you haven't seen him, he said.

I didn't understand at first. No, I then said. Internet. Never saw Steller.

Never?

Never, I said.

He wrote a number on a stamped slip of paper, handed it to me, and said: Forty-seven thirty.

I put the bill in my pocket, took out my wallet, and gave him a fifty, which he shoved in his pants pocket with a sigh. He didn't touch the cash register. It didn't look as though he planned to give me change.

So what's Steller like? I asked.

He almost never comes here anymore. That's why I asked if you knew him.

Where does he live?

He shrugged. He almost never comes here anymore.

The house is new, isn't it?

He laughed, then he began to put my groceries in a plastic bag.

Well, it can't be more than ten years old, I said.

A gift, he said, and put something down in

front of me. It was a small triangle ruler made of transparent plastic, like the ones I had used in school.

Thank you, I said, but our daughter is still too little for—

Try the right angle, he said. Four years!

You mean the house was built four years ago? I was starting to get used to his manner of speaking.

There was a different one there before.

In the same spot?

He nodded. Steller bought it and tore it down and built a new one. You're paying a lot?

Well, yes, I said.

What are you paying?

A lot, I said, took the bag, and turned toward the door.

And the road? he asked.

It's too steep, I said. It's really dangerous. I wonder why they didn't build any barriers.

Good thing no one was coming from the other direction.

How do you know that?

He smiled.

Then I understood. The road leads only there, right? Only to our house!

He smiled.

What was there before? Before the old house that was there before the new one, what was there?

He was silent, and it wasn't clear whether he wasn't saying anything because he didn't know the answer or because he for some reason didn't want to answer.

Goodbye, I said, and after a moment's hesitation, I walked out.

Next to my car stood the woman who had been in the store a short while ago. Because of her dark glasses I couldn't tell where she was looking.

Do you think we'll get snow? I asked.

She didn't reply.

It's definitely unseasonably warm, I said. In December there should be snow on the ground up here, right?

Get away quickly, she said.

What?

Quickly, she said. Quickly get away.

A moment later I was no longer sure whether she hadn't said something completely different or merely cleared her throat, how could anyone tell with that dialect! I waited, but she didn't say anything else. In her glasses I saw my reflection. Then I nodded to her, got in the car, and started the engine.

The drive up wasn't as bad as the drive down. The sun was now halfway behind the rocky ridge between the glaciers, the short winter day nearing its end, the valley lying in shadow, but farther up the green slopes were still shining. I noticed things that I hadn't seen earlier: a pile of stones next to the ruined barn, a rusted-out tractor, the long shadow that the car cast along the road in front of me. A flock of little birds fluttered up out of a bush like an explosion, their bodies rose, were caught by the wind, whirled away. A cloud glowed deep orange. Soon I arrived at the house, put the groceries in the fridge, and sat down at the table to write.

Jana enters the store. Fehringer is standing behind the counter. She takes out the shopping list.

J: Butter, eggs, bread . . .

F: You're not from here, are you, ma'am?

No, he doesn't call her ma'am, obviously. And it has to be terser.

F: You're not from here.

Just a weary observation. Not a reproach, not a question. Get away. He says it like a regrettable cosmic fact, about which there's nothing to be done. Then he grunts and goes out.

Jana's face in close-up.

It's happening again.

It must be an optical

But it's not stopping. I see it. And still see it. Write it down. Have to take a picture of it, but I don't know where my phone

So: I'm sitting at the long table, it's getting dark outside, the reflection of the room can be seen very clearly: fridge, stove, kitchen table, the door to the hall, the flat-screen TV, the low gray-green sofa, the lamp over the table, the table itself, the chair in front of it. I also see the plastic bag from which I just unpacked the groceries, it's lying crumpled on the kitchen table. I see an empty glass next to the crumpled bag—here in the room, there in the reflection.

Only I don't see myself. In the room in the reflection there's no one.

Slowly, look closely. If you look closely and write everything down you will

I shouldn't be able to see the handle of the living-room door, I'm sitting between it and the windowpane, I should be blocking it from view, but there it is! And the back of my chair can be seen, and the tabletop on which I'm leaning. And the open notebook. I cover it with my hand. It should no longer be visible. And yet I see the whole thing. The room that is reflected in the windowpane is unoccupied. Like the day before yesterday. Except that the day before yesterday it was only a moment, this time it's not stopping.

It's still happening.

Still.

It stopped. I stood up to look for the phone and take a picture of it, looking away briefly in the process, and when I turned back to the windowpane, I was in the room. I sat down, my reflection did the same. I wrote *It stopped*. I'm sitting here and writing, I'm sitting there and writing too. There must be an explanation. If I were a physicist, I'd probably know what it is, and all this wouldn't surprise me. But I feel dizzy. Even though it just happened, it seems to me as if it were a long time ago, and I know that in a moment I'll no longer be sure whether it really happened. Write it down so that you remember, so that you can never claim it was only your imagination.

But even as I'm writing this, I'm thinking that it must have been my imagination.

Ella in the car, cheerful and relaxed, she's whistling to herself. Music from the car radio. The phone rings, she presses a button, we hear the voice of the caller, Martin.

M: When are you coming?

E: Be there soon.

M: *When* will you be here?

E: Soon.

M: Yes, but when is that? What does *soon* mean?

(Her face darkens. She turns off the music.)

E: *Soon* means soon!

M: Where exactly are you?

E: In the car.

M: And where is the car?

E: On the road.

M: Obviously it's on the road, but which road and where exactly?

E: (very annoyed) That's hard to answer,

the car is moving and therefore technically always somewhere else.

M: Oh really, it's technically always somewhere else?

E: Is this how you speak to the people you audit?

M: What?

E: Is this how you speak to—

M: If you want to know whether I speak this way to people when I'm conducting a tax audit of their accounts, the answer is no, if only because I don't conduct audits myself. As you might have known by now, I run the appeals department.

E: The appeals department.

M: That's right, people can lodge appeals with us. If we were to audit you, for example—

E: Is that a threat?

M: Ella!

E: You're threatening me with a tax audit?

M: Don't give me any ideas, but

———

It can't be true. Simply can't be.

Because the dream was preying on my mind, I remembered the picture of the woman with the close-set eyes in the laundry room, and I wanted to see it again and went there, *and it's not there!*

I've always thought that when people say something makes their hair stand on end, it's just a figure of speech. But that's exactly how it felt. The picture isn't there, even though my memory tells me clearly that it should be there. And not only is there no picture next to the washing machine, there's also no nail in the wall, not even a hole from a nail. And there's no other picture hanging there either, or anywhere else in the room or in the hall outside it or, now that I think about it, anywhere at all in the house. Everywhere white walls, not a photo, not a painting.

Martin: Don't give me any ideas, but kidding aside—

Ella: Did you really just say *kidding aside*?

M: I wouldn't even be allowed to audit you, but—

E: Don't frighten me like that!

M: —why would that be so bad for you?

E: Why would a tax audit be bad for me?

M: After all, it's only an audit. Like a traffic check. If you have nothing to hide—

E: What are you implying?

M: Nothing, I'm just surprised.

E: You're surprised?

M: Yes, I'm surprised.

No stars, no lights in the valley either. There's only a train flashing by. Susanna has already gone to bed.

At dinner she asked me twice: What's the matter? What was I supposed to say? I said: Nothing, why? And because she looked at me so critically, I added: But what's the matter with *you*? To which she replied: Nothing, but you're acting strange! And because I can't stand that tone, I said: No, *you're* acting strange!

Meanwhile Esther was telling us about a

friend from preschool who is named either Lisi or Ilse or Else and either took a toy away from her or gave her one, at which point the teachers did either nothing at all or just the right thing, or something wrong; little kids are not good storytellers. But Susanna and I exclaimed That's great! and Incredible! and How about that! and the relief when she stopped talking brought us closer together.

Then I carried Esther upstairs, and I briefly had trouble with the bathtub: When I reached for the faucet, it was—how can I describe it? It was farther back than it should have been. I extended my arm, and yet my hand, which should have touched the faucet, since it was only a foot away from my face, was still *in front of* the faucet; I couldn't reach it. Esther giggled. I closed my eyes, took a deep breath, opened my eyes again, and now it worked: I ran water into the oval designer bathtub and listened to its full-toned flow while Esther explained something to me about either Fozzie Bear from *The Muppet Show* or SpongeBob. Really? I exclaimed, and Oh wow! and Oh yeah! Then I put her in the water and washed her and lifted her out again and dried her off, drying the inside of her ear with a corner of the towel, not because it was necessary but because she liked it, and, while she talked and talked, put on her colorful pajamas, which are her favorite ones because there are dinosaurs on them, and carried her down the corridor into her room with its green and violet circles on the wall and an obviously brand-new teddy bear on the shelf, which either another renter forgot or the attentive Steller placed here. Until now Esther had found all this wonderful, but tonight she didn't like it anymore.

Why not? I asked. What's bothering you?

I don't want to be alone here.

But we're next door. We can hear you. We even have this here. I pointed to the camera of the baby monitor. You're not alone here.

Alone in the room.

What's so bad about that?

When you're alone in a room ... She reflected. Then everything is different.

In what way?

When you talk, just you hear it.

And?

That's weird!

Something about that made sense to me. I gently covered her up and dimmed the light to a faint glow with the help of the glass touch-control switch.

If you had another kid, said Esther.

Yeah?

You would love the other kid just as much.

But I don't have another kid.

You would say that to the other kid.

I reached for a picture book, the millipede Hugo's exciting journey God knows where. I read for a while, but she still seemed absent.

What's the matter?

Bad dreams, she said.

You won't have bad dreams.

Yes, I will.

But as I read on, she relaxed and smiled as if to herself. After a few minutes she was asleep. I carefully gave her a kiss on the forehead.

Susanna was talking on the phone when I entered the living room. She hung up and said anxiously that she needed a better agent.

Yes, I said, that's true. I knew that she would never get a new agent, but she would also never stop complaining about her agent. It's the sad truth, and only because I'm certain that she'll never read this here can I say it: Once you're over forty, the roles become sparse. Some actresses can keep going. But most can't.

Luckily she dropped the subject, and we talked about things that people who are raising a child together always have to discuss: the new preschool teacher, whom neither of us likes, and Susanna's father, who wants us to visit him, and my father, who would like to be left in peace, although he would gradually need help, and her friend Sigrid, who was getting divorced, which we considered a mistake. Then we were silent, and I grasped her hand, but she said: Not tonight, I'm tired. And I said: Yeah, the mountain air does that, I'm tired too.

Ella in the car. After the fight she turns off the speakerphone. Then she brakes, pulls over, and turns around. Get away get away get away before get away it's get away too get away late get away

Jana in her new apartment on the couch, Ella storms in. Jana looks up from her laptop.

E: You can't imagine what just—

J: (wearily) Go on, tell me.

E: First he asks me where I am, and I answer

December 5

Susanna and Esther are still asleep. I'm alone in the living room. The sun is about to rise. Where are these dreams coming from?

Give it a try. One thing at a time.

My hands are trembling.

Again the empty room, the lightbulb on the ceiling, no window. Or actually a small window with bars. Wrong, no window. But in the corner the chair with the broken-off leg. And the woman with the narrow eyes. No, it wasn't her, or to be precise: It was her only briefly, then it was Susanna. I ran out the door, down the corridor, and couldn't find the light switch and thought quite clearly that you don't need light in a dream anyway. I just wanted to get out. To get away. I wanted to get away so desperately that I said to myself: Get away, get away, get away. And the woman with the narrow eyes, because it was her again now, was next to me, and I thought: Just don't look at her.

Then I flung open the front door and was outside in the cold. I felt the grass under my bare feet, and the wind hurt my face so badly that I woke up from it.

Susanna was sleeping next to me, the screen of the baby monitor showed our daughter. She was sitting up and looking into the camera, her eyes gleaming white.

But at the same time I still felt the grass on my feet and the wind in my face, and while I was lying in bed, I was at the same time outside, freezing and groping for the door handle, and this wasn't still part of the dream, it was really happening. I found the handle, but the door had clicked shut, I was locked out.

I could hardly breathe. I felt that I could freeze to death. I had to do something fast to get into the warm house, and there was a simple solution: I got up out of the bed. I avoided

looking at the screen again, and ran out of
the room, down the corridor, past the door to
Esther's room. I searched for the light switch,
now I needed it, because I was awake, after all,
and could hurt myself, because the railing of
the staircase was too low, but I didn't find it, so
I could only feel my way slowly, and as a result
I doubled over outside from the cold; I clapped
my hands and jumped up and down, but the
wind bit into my skin, everything went black,
and yet when I had finally reached the door, it
became clear to me that I was not permitted to
open it. It simply was not permitted to happen that I should look myself in the face, from
inside and outside, on both sides of the door,
it was not permitted to happen. I backed away,
and apparently I had done the right thing,
because I felt everything shifting into place; I
was lying in bed again, Susanna was murmur-
ing in her sleep, the monitor showed my daughter soundly sleeping.

So why am I so uneasy? Why are my hands
trembling so badly that my writing is scrawly,

why this pounding of my heart, and why am I still so cold?

In movies a character sometimes realizes that he was only dreaming the bad things, I've used the trick before myself, in *Lola and Uncle*, but the truth is: When you're awake, you know that you're awake. Am I dreaming? is not a question anyone asks seriously. I know I wasn't dreaming.

But I must have been dreaming.

Three acts. In the first Jana moves out of Ella's apartment and has to get by on her own while Ella lives with a man for the first time in her life.

In the second Ella has to learn

The sun is going down. The short winter days in the mountains. We just got back after spending the whole day outdoors.

Even beforehand it was clear to me that a hike wouldn't be a good idea. On the rather long list of things that you shouldn't do with a four-year-old, hiking is very high. But Susanna was bent on doing it.

Are you really sure?

Well, if it were up to you, we'd never leave the house at all!

So after breakfast we put on our down jackets and stuck the little one in the carrier backpack, which Susanna had bought specifically for such outings, and trudged off.

We walked silently and despondently. Glutinous fog refused to clear, the grass seemed colorless, and the oppressive silence was unbroken, except for Esther's chatter. Two hours passed like this. Maybe it was three. Maybe just one. When I listened briefly to Esther, she was talking to herself about a fox and a rabbit and a Mr. Molts or Milts or Malts.

I asked Susanna if she'd ever spoken with the owner of the house.

By e-mail, she said, looking up from her phone. Just a few lines. He was very polite. Why? Is something wrong? The house is lovely!

No, I said, nothing's wrong.

For a while we walked in silence. Even Esther had stopped talking.

Now that you mention it, Susanna said, I do find myself thinking of that movie sometimes. That good movie based on the not-so-good book.

Which movie?

The one with all the Steadicam shots.

Oh yeah, I said, Steadicam. It annoyed me that I didn't know what a Steadicam was. I was a writer, not a cameraman, and I had nothing to do with technology. But it was still embarrassing. So which movie?

Doesn't matter, she said. Not important.

Well, but just tell me which one!

It's really not important.

Why are you bringing it up if it's really not important?

Oh, are we allowed to say only important things now? Otherwise we have to be silent? Like in a monastery?

Now we were both irritated and didn't even know why.

Anyway, something actually is wrong, she said. With the house.

I stopped.

Hard to explain, she said. The atmosphere. Something's not right. I don't sleep well. And have bad dreams, in a really unusual way. The kind of dreams you have when you have a fever. Like, last night we were both in this small room, and you—

Esther pinched my ear, and I was so startled that I cried out. Immediately she burst into tears, and Susanna began to reproach me: How could I be so unthinking, what was the matter with me?

What happened? I asked. In your dream, tell me please!

No, she said. Nothing's more boring than talking about dreams, and anyway, I hardly remember.

What did you dream about? I shouted.

I can't stand it when you're so obsessive.

We walked on. I was no longer in the mood to talk, and Susanna texted sullenly. Esther had fallen asleep. My shoulders hurt from her weight. It began to drizzle.

Do we want to leave? I asked.

Now it was Susanna who stopped. We looked at each other. The rain ran down our shoulders. She stepped toward me, then she threw her arms around my neck.

Today, I said.

Yes, she said. Not one more night here.

Not one more night, I said.

I thought, because your work is going so well. Because you're finally making progress with the screenplay, because you're constantly writing in your notebook!

And I thought that you guys are so happy here.

We're not.

On the way back the rain stopped, the fog cleared, and the mountains rose majestically against the horizon. It almost made you want to stay.

Now she's upstairs packing. And I'm writing for the last time at this table, in front of this window, in front of my reflection, which I hardly dare to look at out of worry that it could disappear again.

What has actually happened? Figments of the imagination, bad dreams, a few peculiar reflections. But it's decided: We're leaving.

Esther is sitting on the floor next to me, putting Legos together, and saying again and again: Look, Daddy, look, and I say: Oh yeah, that's great, without any idea what she's referring to. Unfortunately, we paid in advance, and there are no defects on account of which we could demand a refund. On the contrary, the house is in the best condition.

Still, I'm going to call this Steller now. I'd just like to know who the woman in

Now I've

I have to copy them down.

But quickly before

Her phone, it was lying next to me on the table, and I wanted, because she had Steller's, at least I think that she said she had his number in her, so just as I

Just as I took it, a message. Flashing on the screen. I couldn't help

I want to touch you again.

And I'm thinking what people always think, there must be a completely harmless, maybe it's a joke or out of context or sent to the wrong number, a misdirected message, and I take the phone and hear Susanna walking around on the floor above me, and Esther is tugging on my pants leg, and I shout: Not now! and see that the message is from someone named David, no last name, it just says David, and I don't know any David and so I open the messaging app and check whether

I'm

   going to copy them down. The messages
from her

     and from him. I don't want her to know

How much longer are you away? It feels like forever
before I have you in my
I want to be inside you and
And you? Are you thinking about me and about
how we

   I can't
   I can't copy them down.
   I

I miss you so much.
I miss you it's driving me crazy I want to feel how
I can't right now. You know, the kid
I want you like

   No, I can't
   It's enough. There's no harmless
   I'm shaking like

I can't copy them down.

But I shouldn't let anything show, want to find out

I don't know what time it is. I have to pull myself together, have to pull myself together. Writing helps. I have to pull myself together, because Susanna is gone. Esther is asleep upstairs. What am I going to do tomorrow, when she wakes up, what am I going to do, what am I going to tell her?

I couldn't do it. I wanted to keep it to myself and observe her and find out how deep her deception goes. I wanted to watch her lying to me and at the same time think and try to understand. I wanted to compose myself. At first it was going well too.

For about three minutes.

She came downstairs, peeled an apple for Esther, and said: Please carry the bags out, then we can get going. I'll collect these toys here.

I'll get right on it, I said.

And she: What's the matter?

I said: Nothing, why?

To which she said she could see that something was the matter.

And I: Nonsense!

And she: Go on, tell me!

That's when I started to shout. At least I thought I was shouting, but I gradually began to suspect that my voice was just a croak. Immediately after I had begun, she took her telephone from the table with a swift movement. You might as well leave it there, I shouted or croaked, while Esther stared up at me, I've already copied down the messages, here in my notebook. Who is this David? And although I gathered all my strength to push away the thought, it occurred to me that all this made me feel like I'd stumbled into one of my movies. But that didn't make it any better. In a movie it's funny when a life falls apart, because the people say clever things while it's happening, but in reality it's only dismal and repugnant. Do you want to deny it? I shouted, and only when she looked at me seriously and calmly and said that she didn't want to deny it at all did I realize how much I had hoped she would.

Pull yourself together, she said. Think of your daughter. Then she picked up Esther from the floor and said: Time for bed!

The little one began to whine: It was still light out, not even late, she didn't want to, but Susanna gave her a kiss and carried her out of the room.

I sat motionless. I couldn't think, I had no strength. I heard Susanna walking back and forth upstairs, heard her speaking with Esther calmly and maternally.

I opened the notebook. I read the messages, the fragments of messages, the awful sentences that I had copied down, while I fidgeted with something that had been lying on the table. It was the triangle ruler from the village store. From upstairs I heard Susanna singing a lullaby. Because the inactivity was unbearable, I turned the page and drew a straight line. I rotated the ruler and carefully drew another, at a right angle. I positioned the ruler so that it bisected the right angle and drew a third straight line.

The result looked peculiar.

I checked the measurements. The angle below the bisector came to forty, the one above it to forty-two degrees. How was that possible? I measured the right angle again: ninety, of course. I measured the two angles that made it up: The lower one came to forty, the upper to forty-two, so several degrees should have been missing, but they weren't missing, the right angle was a right angle. I measured again: ninety degrees.

It must have been due to my confusion, to the fact that the world was ending. And yet it made no sense. Slowly and carefully I constructed another right angle and checked the measurement: ninety degrees. With two more right angles I completed it into a rectangle. I drew a diagonal. Two angles in the rectangle were now perfectly bisected. But something was wrong. They weren't exactly oblique, more blurry, my eyes couldn't bring them completely

into focus. I placed the ruler against the line
that divided the right angle and measured the
angle below it: forty-nine. I placed it against
the angle above it: fifty-one.

$$
\begin{array}{r}
49 \\
+ 51 \\
\hline
100
\end{array}
$$

I stared at the drawings. Something was dis-
concerting: When you didn't force your gaze to
stay on them, it glided over them as if of its
own accord.

A trick ruler, what else! I held the triangle
up to the light and shut one eye. The right
angle looked unsuspicious and the degree scale
normal, no numbers were missing. Out of
the corner of my eye I noticed that someone
was standing in the doorway. I started. It was
Susanna. For a moment I had forgotten her.

The phone, how obvious, she said, as she
placed the baby monitor on the table. When-

ever you hear about people getting caught, it's the cell phone, because they couldn't bring themselves to delete the damn messages. She brushed her hair back and gave me an exhausted look. Of course, she said, you think you would be smarter. You consider yourself clever, and then you develop such a ridiculous attachment to those saved messages that you can't bring yourself to delete them. Like all the other idiots. You keep the thing with you at all times and never leave it lying around, but you underestimate the tenacity of the jealous husband, who swipes it from your bag. And the way things stand, you can't even fault him for his jealousy. She sat down and rested her head on her hands.

I said in a shaky voice that I absolutely did not steal her phone from her bag. Something like that never would have occurred to me. It had been lying here on the table, and I had wanted to find this Steller's—

Nonsense, she said. She never would have

just left it on the table. She stood up, looked at me for a long time, and said in an actor's voice: You went through my bag.

I stood up too, felt the blood rushing to my face. I had just enough air to yell: That's absurd, and besides, I'm not the one who has to justify himself—but at that very moment we heard Esther's voice from the speaker. She was sitting up in bed. Susanna ran out. Seconds later I saw her on the screen, kneeling next to the bed and singing.

I sat down. I felt like everything inside me had turned to stone. I didn't know how much time passed. Finally, she came back.

Of what happened next my memory has retained only fragments. I see myself shouting and throwing something on the table, I see myself pounding my fist on the table. She's speaking slowly, she's pale in the face, I'm crying, I'm calming down again. I'm speaking, she's listening silently. I'm asking questions, she's walking back and forth. Then she's the one who is sitting at the table and crying, and I'm standing silently by the window, then I'm shouting at her, but that must be a while later, because the darkness outside is already dense and impenetrable, and then she's shouting too, and I see myself on one side of the table and her on the other, and we're yelling at the same time, but then I'm sitting at the table again and resting my head on my hands and see her leaning limply against the window, and I would like more than anything to stand up and go to her and place my hands on her cheeks and say: Let's forget everything, I love you. But I know that it's not possible, because I can't forget it, and then I go to her anyway and place my hands on her cheeks, but before I can say anything, she says: Just leave me be, leave me be, please leave me be, you don't understand! And then both of us are shouting again, so that I can't listen to her or she to me, and then I'm sitting at the table and hear the front door slamming and the engine starting, and then I'm listening to the faintly rushing silence and have written everything down and still don't understand it, she's right. I don't understand it.

What am I going to do tomorrow when the little one wakes up?

Night, still. Who is this David?

Doesn't matter, I tell myself immediately, it makes no difference. The only important thing is that he exists.

But who is he?

An actor, a dancer maybe, or something even stupider? And immediately I think: What makes you come up with such clichés, you don't know anything about him, he could be a surgeon or a meteorologist. It doesn't matter either. That's not the point.

But who is he?

Maybe one of her colleagues from the last movie, I have to check whether someone named David was involved. But what would that prove? That's not the point.

But who is he?

Tomorrow morning, I have to manage to act in front of Esther as if everything were normal. I have to call the lawyer and ask whether we actually have separate or joint property; crazy that I don't know that, but it's probably still too soon to think about it, I mean, who thinks so quickly about divorce? Though I wonder, on the other hand, how this is supposed to disappear from the world. If I just picture it, her and him, but I'd better not, that's the most important thing: that I don't picture it.

Still night. No idea what time it is. I can't find my phone. I haven't worn a watch in a long time.

I would need the phone too, because it's possible that she'll call.

I have to go back and read it. The past several days, all the lies. I wrote it down, after all. I turn back the pages, and there we are in the living room, on the first afternoon, fighting in the old familiar way, and there we are standing at night by the window, as if everything were as always and as if she weren't thinking about him the whole time, and there we are sitting at breakfast, and I describe her eyes, *not actually blue, more turquoise, with a sprinkling of black*, and the phone is lying next to her, and David is writing to her and she to him and he to her and she to him and he to her, while I—why does it say *Get away* there?

I didn't write that. That wasn't me.

But who else, who could it have been, stay calm, who—she must have done it! Especially since she can forge my handwriting, I know that. I turn the page, and there I am driving into the valley to go grocery shopping, while she stays in the house and has time to talk on the phone with David, and there I am coming back—why does it say *Get away* again there? Think logically. If she had written it in your notebook, then how could it fit in the line like that, wouldn't she have been able at most to write it in the margin?

I can't worry about this now, I can't clear it up, I just can't. I turn to another page, read about our hike. In my naiveté I even wrote down that she was constantly texting on her

It must be almost morning. I'll write very quickly, write down what just happened. I have to write it down so that I don't go crazy. Or in case something happens to me. Esther is lying on the sofa. She's asleep again. It was awful.

I was sitting there and reading my notebook and suddenly heard a noise. It sounded like a human voice, only very high, and it formed words that I didn't understand, a singsong, rising, falling, and rising again, like nothing I'd ever heard before. It took me a few seconds to realize that it was coming from the baby monitor. But on the screen I saw Esther fast asleep: her head on the pillow, her hand sticking out from under the blanket, no one with her. I ran out, up the stairs, down the corridor, I staggered into her room and turned on the light. No one there. She was fast asleep. What else. I listened. Everything was quiet.

So light out again, softly close the door,

down the stairs, but as I was walking down the hall to the living room, I heard the voice again, and it spoke words, strange and ancient, half whisper, half sigh, and when I reached the room and saw on the screen a large figure leaning over Esther's bed, I felt my heart stop.

Only then did I see that it was me. On the screen, next to the bed, it was me myself. Apparently a delay in the transmission; it was the image from a minute ago, and what I heard was probably a radio signal, and as I realized that and heaved a sigh, I saw my daughter sit up in bed with a jerk, open her eyes, stare at the figure, which was me, and begin to scream.

I ran up the stairs, stumbled, banged my knee on a step, struggled to my feet, hobbled on, and called: I'm coming, I'm coming! Door open, light on, there she lay, asleep.

I pulled up one of the colorful children's chairs, sat down, breathed heavily, and thought with a clarity as if someone else were speaking to me: *You should have left. Now it's too late.* Slowly I stood up. I couldn't leave Esther alone, but I couldn't sit on the tiny chair for the rest of the night either. So I gently lifted her out of the bed. She murmured in her sleep, then she moved a little to snuggle up closer to me; her face sank into the crook of my neck, I felt her breath warm on my skin. As I went down the stairs, careful not to fall, she began to snore softly. I went into the living room and laid her down on the sofa. With a sigh she curled up.

And that's where she's sleeping now. I've locked the door to the living room. Esther is here, that's all that matters, who or what is up there I don't want to know. Just a moment ago I saw her still on the screen, sleeping peacefully while the strange voice sang to her—and while she undeniably lay next to me on the sofa. It was unbearable. I pulled the plug.

Then I checked the measurements again. For one of the angles the result remained the same, for the other it changed: The lower one is now thirty-nine degrees and the upper forty-one. I've torn the page out of the notebook, crumpled it into a ball, and thrown it away.

My knee hurts from the fall on the stairs. How much I'd like to turn out the light to make the reflection in the window disappear, but the darkness would be even worse. A moment ago I took a brief look at it. Everything was as it should be, I could see myself and Esther, only the door was wide open. The door that I'd locked.

They're only images, I tell myself again and again, only phantoms, they can't touch anything or do anything, not to you, not to her.

It's completely silent. Only my breathing can be heard.

There's a picture hanging on the wall.

A photo in a thin metal frame. It's hanging next to the steel surface of the kitchen cabinet across from the television. It's hanging slightly askew, and it shows a man leaning against a tree. He's wearing a suit, of a sort that can't have been in fashion in a very long time, in his hand he's holding a hat, and his bearded face looks more than somber, it's despairing. The colors have faded. I remember having written down that there are no pictures hanging in the whole house. I could look it up, but I don't want to now. I don't remember that wall, I could have overlooked the picture. But would I have overlooked a picture like that? And I know I wrote down: There are no pictures hanging anywhere in the house. Would I have written that if there had been a picture here?

Eventually the night will end.

How long was I asleep, stretched out on the floor? My back hurts. Still night. Write down the dream.

I stood outside on the slope and looked into the valley. Then I looked up, above the glaciers, and saw the other mountain.

It was immense, and the drop from it was deeper than any abyss I had ever seen. You could have fallen for hours before you reached the ground, past cliffs and even more cliffs and crevasses and jags and deeper crevasses and more and more rock, and all this got lost in a distance that made me dizzy. While I stared at it, I felt a pull—a weak suction that felt like a current of air, but it was gravity. The mountain had so much mass that you felt its gravity, and I realized that all you had to do was jump and your own weight would pull you toward it and nothing would hold you and you would fall.

And now that I'm sitting at the table and scribbling in my notebook, with aching limbs, the term *World Mountain* comes to me. I don't know what it's supposed to mean, but I can't push it away, because that's what it is; that's what I saw.

December 6

Hurry, while Esther is watching her cartoon.

She woke me up at dawn, and of course she immediately wanted to know where Susanna is.

Mommy has to run an errand in town, I said, but this is fun, just you and me, this is great.

Why was I sleeping on the sofa?

Because that's also fun now and then, sleeping on the sofa!

Why is that fun?

Wait here, I said, I have to look for my phone.

On my way out I looked at the white wall next to the kitchen cabinet. The picture of the man next to the tree was hanging there, as if it had always been there.

As I was going up the stairs, I heard Esther calling for me again.

Be right there, I called, and went into the master bedroom. There were the packed suitcases, she hadn't taken anything with her. And here, attached to its plugged-in charger, was my phone.

I called Susanna, she didn't pick up, I didn't leave a message. More importantly, I had to call a taxi. Even here in seclusion there had to be taxis, if not down in the village, then in the next one, if not there, then in another; as long as I could pay for it, someone would come and get us.

When I returned to the living room, my phone vibrated. On the screen it said *Schmidt*. I hesitated. But since I couldn't afford to displease him, I picked up.

Well, he asked, how are the two beauties doing?

At first I didn't understand, but then I realized that he meant Jana and Ella. They're fantastic, I said. Endless ideas. Already a whole notebook full.

Esther tugged on my pants leg. I pushed her away. She began to cry.

Fabulous, said Schmidt. Really great.

Yes, exactly, I said.

Give me a brief pitch, he said. Tell me.

Not the best moment right now, I said.

Come on, he said, a taste! His voice sounded odd. Could it be that he didn't trust me?

I took a deep breath, opened my mouth, closed it again. Nothing came to me. All the things I had sketched and thought through, all the situations and punch lines were as if erased. I clamped the phone under my chin and opened the notebook—here I was describing how I drove down the road of hairpin bends. I turned the page—here I was buying groceries in the village. Next page, where were Jana and Ella? Be quiet for a minute, I hissed at Esther. Just a minute, Daddy has to talk on the phone, stop crying!

Excuse me? asked Schmidt.

Well, Jana has to move out, I said. Ella

throws her out. Because Martin wants to move in with her.

Martin?

The tax official, don't you remember? That causes problems. Complications. Crazy stuff.

I don't know, he said. When the movie came out I was audited that same month. And again the year after. And what crazy stuff exactly?

Esther was now tugging so hard on my pants leg that I had difficulty keeping my balance.

All different stuff, I said. The craziest stuff.

Well, then say something. Tell me about the crazy stuff!

Can I call you back?

I'm about to meet the people from the funding commission. If you tell me something now, I'll have something that I can—

The reception is bad!

I can hear you fine.

I hung up, then I kneeled down and kissed and hugged my sobbing child. Esther's shoulders jerked, the crying shook her body. Where is Mommy? she shouted.

I told you already, I whispered, and realized with horror that I couldn't remember what white lie I had resorted to.

Where is she?

What was I supposed to say now? If I told her something different from before, she would notice. You know the answer already, I said, lifted her into the air, and whirred like an airplane engine as I heaved her to the right and left and right. She liked that, it actually always worked, and indeed she began to chuckle. The phone vibrated, Schmidt was calling again. I broke out in a sweat, in my fright I whirled Esther with too much force through the air, and again she began to cry.

Sh-sh-sh, sh-sh-sh, I said. It's fun. It's okay. I saw one of her picture books on the floor. I immediately put her down on the sofa, picked up the book, opened it, and began to read aloud. The phone stopped vibrating.

The book was about a stuffed bear who is for some reason named Tumtwimbly, and is searching in a land that is actually a large bed for a golden treasure that really is a golden treasure and was hidden by pirates a long time ago. In a hoarse voice I read:

> *I'll look over there,*
> *said Tumtwimbly Bear,*
> *and I'll look everywhere,*
> *until I behold*
> *the treasure of gold.*

Who writes this stuff, I thought, how do you keep going, how do you live with yourself when you write things like this?

Why is the bear named Tumtwimbly? I asked. What's that about?

Because of his hat, she said.

I looked at the colorful picture. The bear wasn't wearing a hat. I decided to let the matter rest. In the last pages Tumtwimbly Bear doesn't find the treasure, but realizes that there's something more important than riches: that people are good to each other and live together in peace.

But why people? I asked. What does he care about people? He's a bear.

Esther began to cry again.

Do you want to watch TV?

She immediately trembled with joy. Hastily she wiped away her tears. She loves TV more than anything in the world. Normally we don't allow her to watch it, but now was a good time for an exception. I took the remote control and turned it on. The news was on, I changed the channel, the news again, I changed it again, the woman with the narrow eyes. Her face filled the screen.

I turned it off. I was ice-cold, the room seemed to be spinning slowly.

You promised, Esther screamed, why did you turn it off!

Unable to think of any other way to distract her, I jumped up and danced around: Right leg up, left leg up, and I let out a yodel and looked at the distant, gray sky and at the glaciers, which wouldn't help me, and down into the green-gray shadow colors of the valley. For the first time in my life, as I sang and jumped and clapped my hands, I seriously asked myself whether I had gone crazy. But how could you know that, how could you figure it out? Wasn't the very fact that I asked myself the question proof that I hadn't? I clapped and jumped, and Esther, who in her astonishment had forgotten about watching television, mimicked me. No, I thought, it's not that simple. The fact that I'm thinking about it proves nothing.

When Esther was tired, I searched through the contents of the garbage can in the kitchen: apple peels, clumps of oats, small lakes of milk, greasy tinfoil—and there was the crumpled bill from Gruntner's General Store. Address and phone number were stamped at the top of the slip of paper. I took my phone and dialed.

It rang for a long time. Five, six, seven times. It kept ringing. I had been afraid that Esther would cry again, but she just looked at me questioningly. Now it had already rung twelve times. Thirteen, fourteen. Just as I was about to hang up, he answered.

It's me, I said. I need a taxi. Someone has to get us.

Who is this?

What did you want to show me? I asked. With that triangle, what did you want to show me?

Show? he said. Show? Then he was silent for a while.

Yes, they don't fit together, he finally said, right? They never fit, the angles, up there.

But why?

Someone from here . . . He was huffing. It was audibly hard for him not to speak dialect. Someone from here, Hans Ägerli, who owns the Lindenhof, he said an ant doesn't know what a cathedral is or a power plant or a volcano. He coughed, then he said thoughtfully: But Ägerli has been drinking again. He says a lot of things.

What was here before? The house is new, but it has its own road, when was that made?

There was a different house before.

I know, but what sort of house?

Don't shout like that. A different one. Also

a vacation house. People came, vacationed, left again. Often left early. That's why Steller always takes payment in advance. Once something happened.

Daddy, Esther called. I want to show you something!

What happened?

Daddy!

Not now. What happened?

Someone disappeared. A vacationer was there. Then he wasn't there anymore. Was never found. Probably fell off. That happens fast in the mountains. All the crevasses. The smooth slopes. Our paths aren't well marked. Ägerli is responsible for the mountain rescue service, but as you know, he drinks. And people have always disappeared here. In the past too.

What was here before the old house?

A different one.

What sort of house?

Just a different one. And at some earlier time there was a tower there, they say.

A tower?

Or maybe not. That's a legend. But the road is very old.

How old?

It has always been there.

Always?

Always.

And what sort of tower?

The devil built it and a wizard destroyed it, with God's help. Or the other way around, a wizard built it, and God destroyed it.

Is the legend recorded somewhere? Is there a village chronicle?

What?

Village chronicle.

He laughed. We don't have a village chronicle.

Daddy, Esther called. Daddy, now look, look, Daddy!

Her voice sounded so piercing and urgent that I went cold with fright, but she just wanted to show me something that she had made out of Legos.

Really great, I whispered. Really wonderful!

Esther bent down and began to untie my shoelaces.

I have a customer here, he said.

Wait, I cried. I need a taxi! I need a number!

What am I, information?

My wife left with the car. I need a taxi service. I need someone to——

The sound that interrupted me was unlike anything I had ever heard. It was half clang and half snort. It didn't sound like electrical interference, more like something alive.

Hello! I cried. Can you hear me?

But on the phone it was silent, and the screen indicated: No network.

I raised the device, I lowered it, I went to the window. No network. I tied my shoelaces. Come on, I said, and took Esther by the hand. With small steps she followed me. I pushed down the handle, the door was locked. It took me a moment to remember that I had locked it myself last night. The key was in the lock, I turned it, we went out.

Esther squealed with surprise. We were back in the living room.

Indeed, we had left the living room, but the door through which we had gone had led us back into the living room.

Well, how about that, I said with all the cheerfulness I could feign. Then I turned on the movie that I had stored on my phone for emergencies like train trips or restaurant visits, *The Jungle Book*, the old animated movie, and handed her the device. She grabbed it gratefully.

I didn't know where it came from, but I had the vague idea that things would settle down somewhat—the way agitated water smooths itself out when you wait a little while.

The comparison with the ant isn't good. A better one would be with a creature that is drawn on paper. If it could live, it would live entirely on the paper, on its surface. Now imagine there was a mountain on the paper. If the creature made a circle around the mountain and measured the enclosed area, this wouldn't help it understand what it had in front of it. There would be much more paper than, according to its reason, could fit in the circle. For this creature it would be a miracle.

I've written everything down so that anyone who finds the notebook will know what happened. The thought is too terrible, but it's still necessary to think it. My little girl is sitting there and suspects nothing. She's watching her movie. And later they'll say that these two also disappeared: His wife left him, who knows what was going through his head, and the mountains have a lot of crevasses, you start having bad thoughts, and something happens fast.

Rainy afternoon outside. More and more clouds, fog in the valley, and I can no longer see the glaciers. I'd better plug in my phone. In case we make it out of the house, the battery needs to be charged.

———

Now she has watched the movie three times, the tiger Shere Khan has fled in flames three times, Mowgli has returned three times to the man-village. I pull the plug. The battery is fully charged. No reception. I'll leave the notebook on the table. I'll stand up and take Esther's hand and walk backward toward the door, backward down the corridor, backward out of the house. I don't know why, but I have the feeling that it could help if we walk backward.

If we make it, this is the final entry.

December 7

Or still the sixth? St. Nicholas. Yesterday was St. Nicholas Day, not even the kid thought of that. I don't know whether it's past midnight yet.

Strange that I used to find the sight of the stars soothing. I once read that a lot of astronomers think the universe might be infinite. Full of stars, full of galaxies, going on and on and on, going on literally *forever*.

I don't know why I'm thinking so much about stars now.

Esther is sleeping on the sofa again, after the march she was at the end of her strength. My shoulders hurt. A four-year-old is heavier than you think.

And this infinite universe might be only one of an infinite number of infinite universes, each with different laws. One is unreachable from another, they are strictly separate. Normally.

So in the early evening I stood up, took the phone from Esther, grasped her hand, and said that we weren't allowed to turn around, it was a game. Then we walked backward. We actually did make it into the hall: wooden floor, white walls, on the left the door to the washing-machine room, next to it a half-open door, which I had the feeling hadn't been there before. As we went by, I peeked in. The room was empty, on the ceiling hung a naked light-bulb, in the corner was a wooden chair, which was missing a leg. For a moment I was overcome with the confusingly strong desire to go in, but I resisted and pulled Esther onward.

I have to go potty, she said.

Not now.

Our down jackets hung on the coat rack, I took them with my left hand. Without letting go of Esther with my right, I clamped the jackets under my elbow and felt behind me for the door handle. For a moment I was afraid the door wouldn't open, but it did.

Don't turn around, I said.

No, no, no, Esther said, giggling.

We stepped backward into the open. It was ice-cold. Our breath steamed. I closed the door, then I kneeled down and carefully put the jacket on Esther. With chattering teeth I then put on my own, zipped it, and turned up the collar. Now the child-carrier backpack would have been useful, but it was upstairs in the suitcase.

What are we doing now? Esther asked.

We're going on a little outing.

Walking?

I know, you don't like it. But it won't be long.

We set off.

There's someone in the house, she said.

I looked back. I hadn't turned off the light in the living room; behind the bright rectangle of the large window loomed a silhouette. Someone was standing there with hanging shoulders and tilted head, looking down at us.

Nonsense, I said.

Don't you see it?

There's no one there. Come on.

Now the figure seemed to be standing farther to the left than just a moment ago, and now there was another next to it, and now none at all again, while the front of the house rippled around the window. For a moment the size of the building was completely unclear; it projected far into the distance, pointed and gigantic, but not upward, rather in a direction that I hadn't suspected existed.

The house looks so small, said Esther.

Stop looking at it, I said.

As we walked, I was seized by the image of a woman who would stand at the window in several years or had perhaps stood at a window a long time ago and watched paralyzed with terror as two specters, a man and a child, receded hand in hand into the night.

The window behind us still cast a little light

on the road; from the parking area it could be seen running straight for about another fifty yards. Then came the first bend.

I have to go potty, said Esther.

Here, I said. Fast.

When she was done, we walked on. After the bend it was so dark that we might as well have been walking with our eyes closed.

I pulled out my phone. Fortunately I had fully charged the battery while Esther had been watching her movie. The little flashlight on the back provided enough light to illuminate our way on the steeply descending road. I didn't let go of Esther, her hand was warm in my ice-cold hand.

Where's Mommy?

I told you already.

Where is she?

At home. Where we'll soon be too.

It's so dark!

That's true, I said. But isn't this fun? Isn't it interesting? It's an adventure.

She began to cry.

Tomorrow I'll buy you a Lego set, I said. Whichever you want. It doesn't matter how big. I promise.

Any?

You can pick it out.

For some time we walked in silence. She wasn't crying anymore. We reached the second bend, then the third. Outside the beam of light, the darkness was impenetrable. When I pointed the little flashlight on my phone—which still had no reception—at the roadside, I saw bushes, I saw rocks and some earth. I stared in what I assumed was the direction of the valley, but clouds must have gathered, because not a point of light could be seen. I looked up, but the moon wasn't visible.

Daddy, said Esther. Do you know why—

There was a crunching sound next to us. She cried out, I jumped protectively in front of her, a large body bounded past us on four legs and galloped down the road. Esther was crying. I picked her up and kissed her. Her tears tasted salty.

An ibex, I said. Or something like that. Probably an ibex.

The pirate ship too?

What?

Can I have the pirate ship too? The big one?

Of course. Even the really big pirate ship.

After two more bends, the world was extinguished. So silent and so black was it around us that there seemed to be nothing left but Esther and me and the sound of our footsteps in the biting cold. I began to hum. As I listened to myself, I recognized the melody: *London Bridge is falling down . . .*

Sing along, I said. *Falling down, falling down. London Bridge is falling down . . .*

She tried, but then she stopped, and I could no longer bear the sound of my voice and stopped too, and immediately she was crying again. I picked her up. Her face was warm and wet against my cheek. After the next bend I heard myself panting already, and I had to be twice as careful not to lose my balance.

My greatest worry was the cell phone battery. We needed the light, we had to make it down before it died. I tried to carry Esther in a different way and then in a different way again, each time this brought relief for a moment, but then the pain returned. Before long my muscles were trembling, and my fingers felt like they were going to break.

I want to go home, she murmured.

I sensed her fear, and I knew that she snuggled up to me so tightly because she felt safer with me. The fact that I couldn't do the slightest thing to protect her was hard to bear.

We'll be home soon, I murmured.

Soon I couldn't carry her anymore and put her down. I took a deep breath and exhaled and shook my arms. When I closed my eyes, I saw geometric patterns, which intertwined and grew and turned on their axes. The sight was abhorrent, I quickly opened my eyes again.

No need to cry, I said, picking her up again. We're almost there.

Almost where?

We'll ring the doorbell at some house, I said.

First at the store. There's only one store in the village, the owner is a friend, he must live in the same house. And he has a telephone. From there we'll call Mommy.

The sky now seemed a little brighter, I dimly made out the tree trunks. After the next bend they became more distinct. Between the trunks shimmered the light of a house.

Made it, I said. My arm muscles were trembling from Esther's weight, but now I didn't care. Wasn't that fun, wasn't that great? Was really a crazy thing, right?

She didn't respond. In my relief I took longer and longer strides, I was almost running. I turned off the flashlight. The phone still had no reception. The woods thinned, the road led toward the bright window. I took a few more steps, then I stopped. For a moment I still hoped with all my strength that it was only a resemblance and therefore a mistake: the pointed roof, the wide front door, the empty parking area in front, and the large, illuminated window through which you could see the long table and the kitchen and the open door to the hall. But it was no mistake.

We're back, I said.

What?

Back, I said, and put her down. I felt like I was going to vomit, but I struggled against it, that was not allowed to happen. Not in front of the kid.

But we were going down the whole—

It's complicated, I said hoarsely. I'll explain it to you tomorrow, now you have to go to sleep.

But—

It's really late, I said. Adventure over. Wasn't that fun? Now you have to go to sleep.

But I'm hungry!

No problem, I croaked. The fridge is full. I'll make you something to eat. We're home.

Now she's sleeping on the sofa, I covered her with my jacket.

A short while ago there was a man in the room. He didn't look dangerous, more tired. He wasn't the man from the framed photo, because he didn't have a beard, but I think he resembled the woman with the narrow eyes. I couldn't really tell, because he wasn't standing on the floor but on the ceiling, and he was looking down at me as if he wanted to ask for help. But he was here only briefly, and I'm so exhausted that I might also have imagined him. Just as I might have imagined that the empty room with the lightbulb and the broken chair now had another door on the other side. I saw it as I carried Esther down the hall, the other door was open, and behind it was another empty room with lightbulb and open door and behind that one a third; I saw it for only a moment, which is why I'm also not sure whether there was really something moving on the floor of the third. We were immediately in the living room, and I locked the door.

It's the place itself. It's not the house. The house is harmless, it's simply standing where nothing should stand. I suspect there are more places like this, but the others are probably unreachable, on the sea bottom or in mountain caves in which no one has ever set foot. Or there's really only one here, and the next is light years away in the infinite universe. The thought makes your head reel—not a fictitious but a real infinity, filled with things and creatures and galaxies and galaxy clusters and clusters of galaxy clusters and so on and so on, without an end in either direction. And now and then spots where the substance gets thin.

Words. They don't capture how it really is.

I know now why they all have faces like that. Why they look the way they look. It's because of the things they have seen.

When I close my eyes, I see patterns: Sharply defined, they creep along like insects. The place isn't evil, but it's a trap—like a crevasse out of which you could at first climb, but you see the sky above you and think, it's not dangerous, and so you dawdle and look around because there are interesting crystals there, and when you finally do want to climb out, you realize too late that every movement brings you down deeper.

I think it has to do with consciousness. That's why it doesn't hold everyone with the same strength, me more than the kid, for example; maybe I should have sent Esther down by herself, but maybe that would have been wrong too, how can I know?

I've written everything down. Maybe someone will find it. Otherwise they'll consider it a clear case: Marriage broken, screenplay failed, so he looked for an abyss for himself and his poor kid.

And if they find it?

Well, they'll still think that.

Esther isn't moving. She's lying there completely relaxed. As if freed. Breathing deeply and evenly. There's absolutely nothing I can do.

I understand the thing with the angle better now too. It's not easy to put into words. At least not these words. With new words it would be possible. But why bother? If I say that in addition to the three dimensions you have to imagine another three from the other side, or actually *from within* . . . But to whom am I supposed to explain this? To the others who are here forever too? They've known it for a long time, they already know far more.

But maybe I can warn him, that is, me, that is, the man I just a short while ago was, in this way; maybe call to him through undulating time: *Get away*. Shout at him: *Get away, before it's too late*, whisper it, yell it, that he should stop worrying about his movie and open his eyes and see where he is. Somehow get through to him, keep trying until he hears me, until he reads it, until he sees it, until he understands.

It didn't work. I tried it. I'm still here. So he didn't get away when he still could, so I stayed.

Footsteps on the second floor. But that no longer frightens me. Now I'm afraid of completely different things. Someone was walking down the corridor upstairs, something fell on the floor and shattered with a tinkling sound, then the stairs creaked, then the front door closed. Now it's quiet again.

It's getting light out. How am I going to explain it to her when she wakes up, how am I going to explain it? We have food for another two days, but something tells me that food soon won't be important anymore.

I think I hear

She's gone. I'm alone, my God, she's gone. Now it's time to wait.

I have no watch, my phone battery is dead, and the cable that was on the table just a short while ago is now no longer there. It must have been half an hour already, whatever that means, because time is

Now forty-five minutes. If they don't appear again soon, then they

I think they

———

They made it.

When it got light and Esther was beginning to move in her sleep, on the verge of waking up, I suddenly heard the noise of an engine. I knew immediately what it was, and I knew that I had to be fast. I yanked Esther into the air, pushed open the door, and carried her down the hall, which now, however, was not the one from the living room, but the one on the second floor and, on top of that, much longer than it should have been. I ran past the door to Esther's room, which fortunately was closed, and past the other bedrooms and ran and ran, while she began to stir in my arms and looked around in confusion. The hall expanded, and I ran, stumbled, caught myself, kept running toward the stairs, then I heard a honk outside. Esther stretched drowsily and let out a cry of pain as she banged into a picture on the wall, I heard glass shattering on the floor. I ran and ran and couldn't believe that I was still running, Esther began to whine, suddenly I realized that it could conceivably go on like this without end, but then I reached the stairs after all and hurried down. I flung open the door and lurched outside.

There was my car. The headlights were still on, the windshield wipers jerked, a fine drizzle filled the air. Behind the steering wheel sat Susanna.

She got out without turning off the engine. She was pale, her face was furrowed, and she immediately began talking: She had been really worried, she had called a hundred times, I couldn't do that, just stop answering the phone, you didn't do that when you had a child together!

I opened the rear door and put Esther on the backseat. She looked at me wide-eyed. I leaned forward and gave her a kiss. Her cheek was hot. She had a fever. I opened my mouth to say something to her, but nothing occurred to me. There was nothing that was appropriate. So I closed the car door.

He's not important, said Susanna. I don't care about him. He means nothing to me, I never want to see him again.

It took me a moment to understand whom she was talking about.

It was a mistake, she said, a horrible mistake.

Start driving, I said.

But—

I need some time to myself now, I said. I can't talk. I have to think. Yeah, I have to think. About everything.

But not here!

It's good here, I said. I like it here, it's a good place to think. About everything. Please drive now. Drive fast! I'll get in touch. Drive.

She opened her mouth to speak.

No, I said. Trust me. Start driving!

She nodded.

When we looked at each other, I felt split into two beings. The knowledge that I would never see her and Esther again was unbearable. But at the same time they were both so

far away from me that I didn't know whether I
would have even wanted to return to the place
to which I could not return. I put my arms
around my wife, and I felt as if someone else
were doing it, someone with whom I shared
only a name. What was the name again? I tried
to remember. We held each other for several
seconds. Already too long. I let go, pushed
her away from me, stepped back, and said in a
trembling voice: Go!

She nodded and got in the car. It started to
move, went around me, and drove away. For a
moment I saw Esther's face, pale in the rear
window, then they had disappeared around the
bend. For a while I still heard the engine noise.

The rain ran down my head. I looked up at
the house. How different it looked now. Slowly
I went in.

That's all there is to report. The water is draw-
ing its rain lines on the window. The clouds are
so dense that I can see the room very clearly in

the reflection again—the long table, the cabinet, the kitchen, the door. There's no one in the
room reflected there. But there's a notebook on
the table.

And yet I'm only at the very

YOU SHOULD HAVE LEFT

Daniel Kehlmann was born in Munich in 1975 and lives in Berlin and New York. His works have won numerous prizes, including the Candide Prize, the Doderer Prize, the Kleist Prize, the Welt Literature Prize, and the Thomas Mann Prize. His novel *Measuring the World* was translated into more than forty languages and is one of the biggest successes in postwar German literature. He is currently a fellow at the Cullman Center for Scholars and Writers of the New York Public Library.

A NOTE ON THE TYPE

The text of this book was set in Van Dijck, a typeface named after the Dutch punchcutter Christoffel van Dyck, c. 1606–69. This revival was produced by the Monotype Corporation in 1937–38 with the assistance, and perhaps over the objection, of the Dutch typographer Jan van Krimpen. Van Dijck nonetheless has the familiar qualities of the types of William Caslon, who used the original Van Dijck as the model for his famous type.

Typeset by Scribe,
Philadelphia, Pennsylvania

Printed and bound by R R Donnelley,
Crawfordsville, Indiana

Designed by Betty Lew